Abuelita's Heart

AMY CÓRDOVA

SIMON & SCHUSTER BOOKS FOR YOUNG READERS

SIMON & SCHUSTER BOOKS FOR YOUNG READERS

An imprint of Simon & Schuster

1230 Avenue of the Americas, New York, New York 10020

Copyright © 1997 by Amy Córdova

SIMON & SCHUSTER BOOKS FOR YOUNG READERS

is a trademark of Simon & Schuster.

Book design by Heather Wood

The text for this book is set in Schneidler Medium.

Printed and bound in the United States of America.

First Edition

1   3   5   7   9   10   8   6   4   2

Library of Congress Cataloging-in-Publication Data

Córdova, Amy.

Abuelita's Heart / by Amy Córdova. — 1st ed.

p.   cm.

Summary: Before returning to the city with her parents, a young girl walks
with her grandmother, learning about the special feelings, places, and plants
that are part of her heritage and the Southwestern desert where Abuelita lives.

ISBN 0-689-80181-5

[1. Grandmothers—Fiction. 2. Southwest, New—Fiction.] I. Title.

PZ7.C81537Iae   1997   [E]—dc20   96-12082

With special thanks to my mother, Viletta Sprangers — A.C.

• *A note from the artist* •

*I used acrylic paints, oil pastels, colored pencils, and a very big eraser on
Stonehenge paper to create the illustrations for this book. After months of
preliminary sketches I traveled to a secluded casita on Pot Creek, where I stayed
with my elder artist friends Jim and Russie, and made these pictures. My heart has
long been filled with awe in witness to the history and strength of my relatives in
this splendid place I now call home . . . here, in northern New Mexico.*

With thanks to my Abuelitas,

Valera Munro and Josephine Córdova,

whose love shone like beacons in my young life.

And to Abuelitas everywhere.

MY ABUELITA LIVES IN A LAND the color of sunset, where each day the great sky herds woolly clouds over the mountains to far-off pastures. Abuelita says, "The earth is enchanted here. La tierra está encantada aquí."

The dusty path to Abuelita's weaves across the canyon like a drowsy red snake. Even though I'm wearing the beaded moccasins that Abuelita made, my steps feel heavy and slow. It is as though my feet want to remember each turn of the trail that leads me to my Abuelita.

Tomorrow, my parents and I will fly away in a big plane and return to our home in the city. Today, I see Abuelita's adobe casita rising from the earth. Her home is made of sunbaked bricks of mud, sand, and straw and is painted the color of blooming cactus flowers.

My moccasins pat the ground in soft drumbeats.

Cristál, Abuelita's silver dog, rises on stiff legs to greet me.

"Hola perrita, mi amigita. Hello little dog, my dear friend. Como estás hoy día? How are you today?"

The curtain flutters and my heart feels like a jar of butterflies. Suddenly, the wooden door swings open, and she is there!

Abuelita, my grandma!

"Corazoncito mío, my dear heart," she sings.

Our hug is big and round, and inside it, the whole world!

Urraca, the magpie, has been listening from a hidden perch in the old pine. He peeks out and squawks a rusty "Hello." Lagartija, a tiny lizard, sunning herself on the warm adobe wall, is startled by Urraca's loud cackle, and streaks off to a new hiding place under the Maravilla bush. A rabbit, un conejo, bounces out from behind the bush, followed by three small ones, hopping like popcorn.

"Goodness me," laughs Abuelita, "so many are waiting for you today, Corazoncito, and all of them relatives!"

A little breeze whistles sweetly. The old trees sway to the tune as the heat of the afternoon fades. At Abuelita's, all things seem to be awake.

Encantadas…enchanted.

At suppertime Abuelita says, "Corazoncito, are you ready for your happiness meal?"

We laugh as she fixes us each a bowl of sopa de frijoles con salsa verde. "Mi favorita, my favorite!"

Our soup is made of pinto beans and green chilies. Abuelita winks. "Being together makes any meal happy." Cristál and I agree.

Abuelita and I sing "Cielito Lindo," a song to the Pretty Sky as we clear the table and tidy the cocina, the kitchen.

Then, Abuelita takes down her walking stick and opens the big door. "Come, ven, Corazoncito, tonight is an important one for us."

Cristál is waiting. With an eager wave of her plumed tail, our twilight journey begins.

"Grandfather Sun is my favorite artist," sighs Abuelita. "See how he paints the earth with His golden glow?"

We walk hand in hand as night creeps across the high desert. White-fringed wings sweep the sky in silence as Urraca and his clan return to the algondones, the cottonwood grove that is their home. Abuelita tells stories of the healing plants, her remedios, that grow everywhere around us.

"Mira, look, Corazoncito. We call these that grow near the arroyo, the stream, yerba buena, the good herb. Their fragrant leaves make a tasty mint tea to cure the stomachaches.

"And see the yucca plant, Corazoncito? The roots make a sudsy shampoo to clean your hair.

"Now, here is my special plant, the sage, chamiso…just the medicine to clean and heal both body and spirit. After the rains, you will know the chamiso by the strong perfume it wears."

Then, Abuelita sprinkles blue cornmeal on the ground to thank Mother Earth for loving us so much. "Bendito sea," hums Abuelita. "Blessed be."

The lavender hues of twilight deepen to reveal the great star blanket of night. "Did you know, Corazoncito, that the stars are really the campfires lit by those who have left this Earth and are making their way back home to the Creator?"

In awe, I gaze at the flickering lights. In the distance, coyote sings the moonrise song. "Beauty is everywhere, Corazoncito…everywhere."

As we make our way, Abuelita unwraps a candle and lights it.

"Come. Ven, Corazoncito."

The candle's pale light invites us to a slim opening in the canyon wall. I see a doorway!

Together, we step inside.

"This old cave keeps safe a precious gift left by our ancestors, a gift that belongs to you, too, Corazoncito." Abuelita motions to a spot high on the wall.

A heart, carved deep into the rock, shines in the wavery glow of the candlelight.

"I have shown you my remedios, the healing plants that grow outside, but here, on the inside, is the greatest healer on Earth," whispers Abuelita. "Bienvenida, welcome, Corazoncito mío, to the Cave of the Heart. La Cueva del Corazón!"

"I first came to this place with my Grandpo when I was young like you. My Abuelo gave me the gift of the corazón, and tonight I offer that same gift to you.

"The old heart may not look like much, Corazoncito, but don't let it fool you. It is life's most precious treasure. Here, aquí. Adentro, inside." Abuelita pats her chest and smiles gently.

"Know that your relatives are all the beings who share this Earth," Abuelita says softly. "See how the spirals of the heart reach out, giving themselves one to the other? It is by reaching out to one another that we, too, create something beautiful to last throughout the ages. No matter where life leads you, Corazoncito mío, if you follow the heart your path will be one of wonder."

Outside again, the air has caught a chill. Abuelita covers us with her rebozo, her shawl. We lie on the earth to take in the night's splendor. Cristál flops down with a sigh and curls herself around us.

Snuggled into Abuelita's warm embrace, I am comforted by the rise and fall of her breath and the perfumed sage on her hands and clothes.

As we lie under night's velvet blanket, I float off into a dream.

I see myself, my Abuelita, my Papa and Mama. We are shining like candles in the glow of the heart. Each one of us has a light that reaches out and mingles with the others, causing great warmth and brightness among us.

I watch as the light reaches out and touches my family and friends. The light beams in their faces and then returns to shine on us. The light of the corazón twinkles in the night sky for those who have left us to walk the star path home.

It grows bigger and stronger as it shines, connecting one being to another, until the world is spilling over in brightness.

Happiness, like my dream, swirls around me.

Tomorrow, I will take something precious with me back to my home in the city, something I will share. I have my Abuelita's strongest remedio…the corazón!

"Treasure the gift, Corazoncito mío. May it shine in you like Grandfather Sun." Abuelita's words are soft like her prayers.

I reach out and Abuelita's warm hand is in mine. Love is everywhere, and the moon shines bright upon us.

ABUELITA'S RECIPE FOR LA COMIDA DE ALEGRÍA

The Happiness Meal

2 cups dry pinto beans

3-4 cups vegetable broth

1 tbsp. fresh chopped garlic

1 tbsp. ground cumin

1/4 cup chopped mild green chilies
   (you can use a small can, but fresh is better)

fresh cilantro

grated Monterey Jack or cheddar cheese

sour cream

salt and pepper, to taste

Cover the beans with water, add a dash of salt, and let them soak overnight.

In the morning drain the beans and replace the water with enough vegetable broth to cover the beans plus one to two inches. You'll need to add more broth as the beans cook. Add garlic and cumin. Cook slowly over low/medium heat until the beans soften. Add chilies, salt, and pepper.

Cook one half hour more until beans are quite tasty.

Top with fresh cilantro, grated Monterey Jack or cheddar cheese, and sour cream.

Serve with fresh warm tortillas or tortilla chips.

OPTIONAL: You can substitute chicken broth for vegetable broth and/or add one cup cooked shredded chicken.

The secret ingredient to a happiness meal is sharing it with someone you love.